Up the Dizzy Mountain

written by Kaye Umansky
illustrated by Steve Smallman

The Story So Far ...

The friends are determined to rescue Obby the Obbygobulum, who has been captured and taken to Giant Gong's castle, up the Dizzy Mountain. They have been helped by Wizard Wagoo, who gives them magical gifts to help them on their way. Pip chooses to take Dougal, the wizard's little dragon, to show them the way and Wizard Wagoo gives them two tandems to ride. But the Gungees chase them on scooters. Luckily, the lift appears in a cloud and once again the children escape.

Now read on ...

Chapter One

Snow!

"Are we ready?" said Sam. Her hand hovered over the magic button.

"As ready as we ever will be," said Jojo, with a gulp.

"Hooray!" cheered Pip. "Want to see Dougal!"

This time, there had been no talk about whether or not they would go back. Everyone knew that they were in too deep to back out now. But nobody was looking forward to it. Only Pip was smiling. He had made a terrible fuss about coming too. The others had finally given in to him, although they weren't too happy about it.

"Wait!" said Ben, suddenly. "The letters have changed, look. It doesn't say W. W. any more."

He was right. Two new letters glowed by the side of the button.

"D. M.," read Jojo. "What can that stand for?"

"Dizzy Mountain," said Mouse. "That's what comes after the Wild Woods, isn't it? We saw it from the air, remember?"

"Looks like we're getting nearer to Gong's castle, then," said Sam. And she pressed the button.

The doors opened – and everybody's eyes grew wide.

"Wow!" gasped Ben.

"Snow!"

"Whoopee!" cheered Pip. "Want to make a snowman!"

There was snow all right. Snow as far as the eye could see. They stood on the edge of a frozen lake with fir trees all around. In the distance, behind the trees, loomed an enormous mountain. At the very top, against a grey background of cloud, stood a huge castle.

"There it is," said Sam, pointing. "Gong's castle. That's where we have to go."

"Brrr," said Mouse. It wasn't just the cold that was making him shiver.

"How are we supposed to get up there?" asked Jojo. "We need thick boots and warm clothes. We'll freeze in jeans and jumpers. Pip's only got a T-shirt."

"We haven't planned what we'll do when we get there, either," Mouse pointed out. "We haven't even got the things Wizard Wagoo gave us. They vanished when we got home." He put his hand into his jeans pocket. A surprised look came over Mouse's face as he slowly took out a brown paper bag. "It's the Strange Sweets," he said. "That's amazing. I wasn't even wearing these jeans the last time I came."

Everyone patted their pockets. Ben found that he still had his little packet of Sneezing Powder. Sam had her pot of Slippery-Slide Cream.

"No more Flying Dust, I'm afraid," said Jojo, sadly. "I used it all when we were being chased by the Gungees."

5

"Where's Dougal?" asked Pip.

"Flown back to Wizard Wagoo, I expect," Jojo told him. "He wasn't yours to keep, Pip."

"Why?" asked Pip. He sat down in the snow, looking cross. "I want to take him home to show Mummy."

"Hmm," said Jojo. "I'm not sure Mum would like a dragon."

"Yes she would," argued Pip. "I'd keep him in my room. Not fair. You've got a hamster and Mouse has got a rat. Why can't I have a dragon?"

"You just can't," said Jojo. "Now, get up. You'll catch cold, sitting there."

"This isn't getting us anywhere," said Ben, through chattering teeth. He was stamping his feet and rubbing his arms. "We'll just have to go back down in the lift and get our winter jackets. And gloves, and scarves, and ..."

"Ben," said Sam.

"... and thick boots and woolly socks and ..."

"Ben," said Sam again.

"What?"

"We can't go back, Ben. The lift's gone."

She was right. It had.

Chapter Two

Buddy

"Now can I make a snowman?" asked Pip, who didn't stay cross for long.

"No!" said the others. He really could be annoying sometimes.

"This is serious, Pip," explained Ben. "We're not here to play games. We've got a big problem."

"Is that a fact?" broke in a cheery voice from behind them. "Anything I can do to help?"

Everyone whirled around. Standing right behind them, leaning against the trunk of a nearby fir tree, was a huge, white bear!

"A polar bear," said Pip, thrilled. "Like on my T-shirt!"

"That's me, little fellow," agreed the bear. "Buddy's the name. Put it there!"

He stooped and held out a paw. Pip stuck out his little hand and shook it.

"That's my brother," said Pip. "He's Mouse. And my sister's Jojo. And that's Ben and Sam. Will you shake their hands too?"

"Sure," said Buddy. "Hey, what's up, kids? Cat got your tongue?"

Again, he stuck out his big, furry paw. Feeling rather shy, everyone shook it in turn.

"That's more like it. Nice and friendly, eh?" boomed Buddy. "Spotted you from across the lake. Don't get many kiddies round here. Not dressed like you lot, anyhow. Don't you feel cold?"

"Freezing," agreed Sam.

"And that's your problem?"

"Well, yes. One of them."

"Say no more," said Buddy, with a little wink. He scooped Pip high into the air, over his head and onto his broad shoulders. "Follow me, boys and girls," he said, and strode out onto the ice.

"Isn't it dangerous?" asked Mouse.

"Not when you're with your Uncle Buddy, kiddo," said Buddy. "I'm an expert."

Rather nervously, the children stepped onto the ice. It felt firm, but very slippery. Clutching onto each other and giggling, they tried to keep up with Buddy, who had no trouble at all, even with Pip on his shoulders.

"I'm having a bear-back ride!" shouted Pip, red with excitement.

"Where are we going, Buddy?" asked Sam.

The huge bear pointed. "See that little shack across the lake? With the smoke coming out of the chimney? That's where the Reindeer Lady lives. She'll dig you out some warm clothes, if you ask her nice."

Mouse was about to ask who the Reindeer Lady was, but instead, he fell down on his bottom for the third time. Perhaps he would leave the questions until later. Slipping and sliding, they continued on their way across the ice.

"There she is," said Buddy. A short, plump figure stood in the doorway of the tiny shack, waving merrily. "Brought you some deep frozen kiddies!" shouted Buddy. "Hope it's warm in there!"

"Warm as toast!" came the cry. "Come on in, and welcome."

The children exchanged smiles. They liked the sound of the Reindeer Lady.

Chapter Three

The Reindeer Lady

"My, my, you'll catch your death of cold," fussed the Reindeer Lady, leading them in. "Give them some blankets, Buddy, while I get them some hot broth."

The children wrapped themselves in blankets and watched while she scurried around. She had bright red cheeks and merry little eyes.

The shack was very tiny, but the glow coming from
a tiny stove made it cosy. Bunches of herbs hung from
the low rafters. There was a hammock in one corner
and fishing rods propped in another.

"There," said the Reindeer Lady, thrusting steaming
bowls under their noses. "Get that down you. I don't
know what your mothers are thinking of, letting you
out without your jackets on."

"Our mothers don't know we're here," said Ben.
He took a spoonful of broth. "Mmm. This is good."

"Came in the lift, they did," said Buddy. He was
so tall, his head nearly touched the rafters.

13

"Oh, I see. You must
be the children we've been
hearing about," said the Reindeer Lady.
Her little black eyes studied them closely.

"You've heard about us?" asked Sam, through
a mouthful of broth. "How?"

"Oh, the word gets round. Not many people are
prepared to stand up to Gong. I hear you've been
having a bit of trouble with the Gungees."

"We certainly have," agreed Ben. And before he knew
it, he found himself telling the Reindeer Lady all about
their adventures so far. The others chipped in now and
again. Pip amused himself by swinging in the hammock.
"... so we've come to rescue Obby. Next stop, the castle,"
finished Ben.

"Well, well," gasped the Reindeer Lady. "You've had
some adventures, and no mistake. It's a good job your
mothers don't know what you've been getting up to."

"Why are you called the Reindeer Lady?" asked Mouse, who had been dying to know.

"Wait and see," she said. She gave a little chuckle. "Finished your broth? Right. Look in the cupboard and find yourselves some warm clothes. There are some fleecy boots in there too. You'll need to wrap up warm. Then I'll take you out and show you something."

The cupboard was stuffed full of thick coats. It didn't take long to find things to fit them, although Pip was a problem, being so small. In the end, Buddy stuffed Pip's boots with newspaper, which made him giggle.

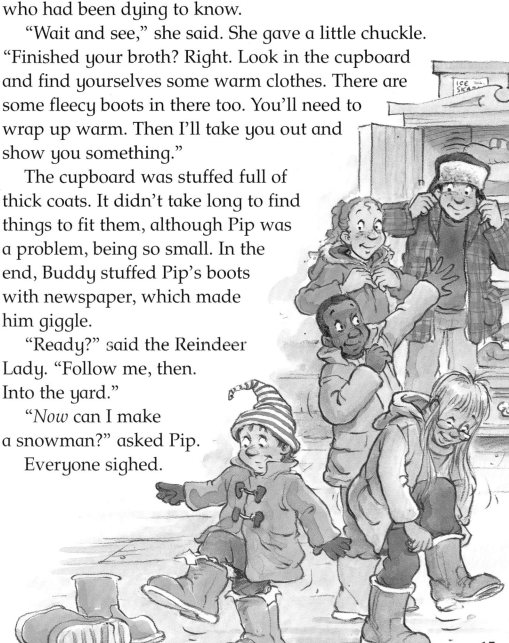

"Ready?" said the Reindeer Lady. "Follow me, then. Into the yard."

"*Now* can I make a snowman?" asked Pip.

Everyone sighed.

Chapter Four

Rusty the Reindeer

The Reindeer Lady led them outside and around to the back of the shack, passing a ramshackle shed on the way. That was when they got another surprise. There, sheltering beneath the trees, stamping their feet and looking up with startled eyes, were …

"Reindeer!" gasped Jojo. "Real reindeer! With antlers and everything!"

"Hooray!" cheered Pip. "Rudolph!"

He tried to run towards them and fell over his big boots. With a chuckle, Buddy set him back on his feet.

The Reindeer Lady gave a little whistle. The biggest reindeer, with huge antlers, came trotting over and nuzzled into her. It wore a bell around its neck, which tinkled softly.

"This is Rusty," said the Reindeer Lady. "Not Rudolph, Pip. He's got a black nose, see? You can stroke him if you like."

"Hello Rusty," said Pip, reaching up to pat his warm neck. He looked into the reindeer's soft brown eyes. "I'm going to make a snowman soon," he whispered.

"Fetch the sledge would you, Buddy?" asked the Reindeer Lady. She took some sugar cubes from her pocket and gave them to Jojo.

"Here," she said, "Give these to Rusty. He'll need sweetening up if he's going to take you up the mountain."

The children's eyes widened. "Really?" said Ben. "He'll take us to the castle?"

"I reckon you'll need all the help you can get," said the Reindeer Lady. Her merry face was suddenly grim. "Your little Obbygobulum friend doesn't know what he started when he stood up against Gong. Brave he may be. Wise he isn't."

Just then, Buddy appeared around the corner, towing a heavy sledge behind him. It was painted blue and white and was piled with thick blankets.

Rusty gave a little snort, then trotted over and stood quietly in front of it. Pip stroked Rusty's nose while Buddy and the Reindeer Lady fixed the harness.

"In you get, then," said the Reindeer Lady, when they had finished. "Make sure you tuck in the blankets. It's cold up the mountain." Eagerly, everyone jumped into the sledge. This was too good to be true!

"Ready?" said Buddy, when they were all in. To everyone's surprise, he picked up the leading rein.

"Are you coming with us?" asked Pip, excitedly.

"Why, sure. Can't let
you do this on your own, can I?"

Huge grins broke out on every face.
So Buddy was coming along to help them.
Suddenly, things seemed a whole lot brighter.

Flakes of snow began to fall as Buddy led
Rusty out of the yard and into the trees.

"Rusty the Black-Nosed Reindeer!"
sang Pip, bouncing up and down happily.

Everybody laughed.

"You take care, mind!" called the Reindeer Lady.

"We will!" called the children. "Thank you!" They
waved until they could no longer see her for trees.

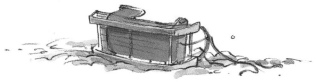

Chapter Five

Sledge Disaster

At first, it was fun. Their warm clothing kept the cold out and the trees provided some shelter against the snow. Rusty had no trouble pulling the sledge up the steep slope. Buddy's strong legs never seemed to get tired. The children joined in with Pip's song.

"This is great!" said Jojo, eyes shining.

Pip leaned over the side and scooped up a handful of snow.

"Don't you dare!" said Mouse.

Too late. He received a face full of the stuff.

That was the signal for everyone to do the same. Giggling and spluttering, they all grabbed handfuls of snow from low lying branches and pelted each other.

Up and up they went, higher and higher. And then ...

"Best be quiet now, kids," warned Buddy. "The trees are thinning out. We're getting near the castle."

Everyone became quiet. Up ahead was a great stretch of unbroken snow, ending at massive iron gates set into the towering castle wall. Behind the wall loomed a huge, stony castle with snow-covered turrets and towers.

"I don't like the look of it," said Mouse.

"How will we get in?" muttered Sam. "It looks impossible. We'll never climb those walls."

"What's that?" said Ben, sharply. "That sound. Is that what I think it is?"

Everyone listened. The colour drained from their cheeks.

It was the howling of wolves!

Then, a terrifying thing happened. The huge gates swung
open in a shower of snow – and dozens of small sledges
came zooming out. Each was painted black and yellow.
Each was pulled by a lean, mean-looking wolf. And worst
of all, each sledge was occupied by ...

"Gungees!" wailed Jojo.

   With wild screams, the Gungees came whizzing down
the steep slope towards them.

   Rusty reared up, front hooves lashing at thin air.

   "Whoa!" shouted Buddy. "Easy, boy!"

But Rusty was too
strong, even for Buddy.
As Rusty turned, one of the
sledge's runners caught in a tree root.
Before they knew it, the children were thrown
out and lying face down in the snow.

"Ahhh!" choked Mouse, spitting out snow. He raised
his head just in time to see the reindeer vanish into the
trees, with the sledge sliding crazily behind him.
"Now what?"

Ben, Sam, Jojo and Pip were struggling to their feet,
confused by the suddenness of it all.

The howls of the wolves and the whoops and screams
of the Gungees were getting closer.

"Over here!" Buddy shouted. "There's a cave! Quick!"

Sure enough, he was standing by the entrance to a cave.
Stumbling and slipping in the deep snow, the children
ran for it.

"Behind me, kids!" ordered Buddy. And he stood
at his full height, blocking the entrance.

The frightened children huddled behind him. Jojo
cuddled Pip, who was crying a little bit.

The leading Gungee reined in his wolf and the sledge
skidded to a stop. The other Gungees did the same. They
formed a line, only a few metres from the cave entrance.
Grinning nastily, the leader climbed from his sledge.
"Back, bear!" the leader snarled. His teeth were sharp and
yellow. "Boss don't want you! Wants children!" The wolf
standing next to him growled and showed its teeth.

"You'll have to get past me first," said Buddy.

Chapter Six

Ben's Idea

"You think you tough, eh?" sneered the Gungee leader. "Right. We soon see how tough you are."

He reached into the sledge and picked up a snowball. He drew back his arm and threw the snowball with all his might.

It hit Buddy's ear and bounced off, landing on the cave floor in a shower of dirty snow. Buddy clapped a paw to his ear and gave a furious roar.

"This is looking nasty," said Sam. "He put a stone in it, look!" As she spoke, more snowballs with stones in came hurtling through the air. The children saw that the Gungees' sledges were piled high with them.

"Cowards!" roared Buddy, as stones rained down on him. "Come closer, if you dare! Cowards! Scaring little kids! I'll – ouch!"

A big stone hit him smack in the mouth.

"Buddy!" sobbed Pip. "They're hurting Buddy!"

"I've had enough of this," muttered Ben. And he ran forward.

"What are you doing, Ben?" shouted Mouse.

"Stay there. I've got an idea!"

"Be careful!" yelled Sam.

"Buddy! Ben!" blubbed Pip, tears streaming down his face.

"Shush, Pip," begged Jojo, cuddling him. "Be a brave boy."

"Get back!" growled Buddy, as Ben appeared at his side. "Nothing you can do, kiddo."

"I think there is," said Ben. He ducked to avoid another stone-filled snowball. "I just want to try something."

He reached into his pocket with trembling fingers – and brought out a small, white packet.

"Right," he said. "Here goes." He ripped it open, held it to his mouth – and blew.

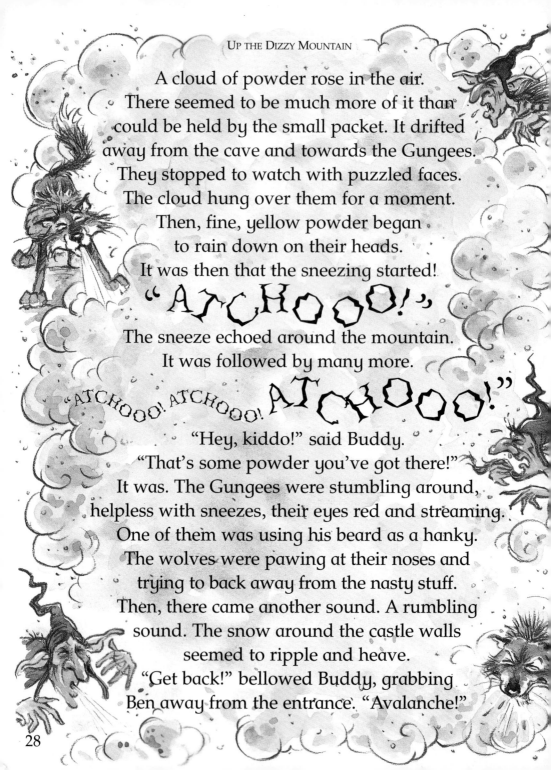

A cloud of powder rose in the air.
There seemed to be much more of it than
could be held by the small packet. It drifted
away from the cave and towards the Gungees.
They stopped to watch with puzzled faces.
The cloud hung over them for a moment.
Then, fine, yellow powder began
to rain down on their heads.
It was then that the sneezing started!

"ATCHOOO!"

The sneeze echoed around the mountain.
It was followed by many more.

"ATCHOOO! ATCHOOO! ATCHOOO!"

"Hey, kiddo!" said Buddy.
"That's some powder you've got there!"
It was. The Gungees were stumbling around,
helpless with sneezes, their eyes red and streaming.
One of them was using his beard as a hanky.
The wolves were pawing at their noses and
trying to back away from the nasty stuff.
Then, there came another sound. A rumbling
sound. The snow around the castle walls
seemed to ripple and heave.
"Get back!" bellowed Buddy, grabbing
Ben away from the entrance. "Avalanche!"

Chapter Seven

Saved!

The rumbling grew louder. The ground beneath their feet was shaking. The children pressed back against the cave walls, with their eyes fixed on the entrance. Then, as they watched, a great, white wave of snow came thundering past.

"Want Mummy!" wailed Pip. Jojo held him close. The rumbling and shaking seemed to go on forever.

Then, very suddenly, it stopped. Jojo looked up at the cave entrance. It had gone. In its place was a great, thick, white wall of snow.

"Hey," said Buddy. "Looks like it's stopped, kids. Our lucky day, eh?" He gave a chuckle.

"I'm not so sure," said Mouse, staring at the snow blocking the entrance. "We'll never dig our way through that lot. There must be tons of the stuff. We can't get out! We're trapped! We ..."

Sam poked him in the ribs.

"What?" said Mouse.

"Look behind you," said Sam.

The lift had arrived. The cave wall had silently split in two, and there it was, doors open, waiting for them to walk inside.

"You see?" said Jojo, "We're saved. Good old lift."

"Well now, will you look at that!" said Buddy, with a grin. He rubbed his sore ear, where the stone had hit him.

"Are you all right, Buddy?" asked Ben.

"Sure, kiddo. No bones broken. Takes more than a stone or two to stop your Uncle Buddy. That was good work there, young Ben, by the way."

"Thanks," said Ben. He suddenly thought of something. "But what about you, Buddy? How will you get out?"

"He can come home with us," said Pip. "He can live in my room."

Buddy gave a great bellow of laughter. "And what would your mum say about that, eh? No, little fellow. The lift is your way home, not mine. Don't you worry about me. There's another way out of this cave. It goes back further than you think. There's a tunnel that leads back down to the pine trees. Bit of a squeeze, but I've done it before."

"So this is goodbye, then?" said Sam, sadly.

"Looks that way," agreed Buddy. He stuck out his paw and everyone shook it in turn. Pip gave him a big hug.

"That's what you call a real bear hug," chuckled Buddy.

"Thanks for everything, Buddy," said Ben. "You've been a good friend."

"Hey! Think nothing of it. Off you go, now. Take care, kiddies."

"We will," promised everyone. And they stepped into the lift. Mouse pressed the button – the doors closed – and down they went.

They stepped out onto the landing. The thick coats and warm boots they had borrowed from the Reindeer Lady had somehow vanished into thin air, and they were wearing their own jeans and jumpers.

"All that," sighed Sam, "and we still haven't rescued Obby."

"We're getting closer, though," said Ben. "Haven't you noticed? Each time we go, we get nearer. I've a feeling that next time, the lift will take us straight to Gong's castle."

"I don't want to think about that right now," said Mouse. "I've had quite enough excitement for one day. What's the matter, Pip? Why are you looking so cross?"

"Never made a snowman," sniffed Pip. And he stomped off to play with his robot.